FLASHBACKS

# DEAR MUM, I MISS YOU!

## STEWART ROSS

FLASHBACKS

# DEAR MUM, I MISS YOU!

## STEWART ROSS

Illustrated by
LINDA CLARK

EVANS BROTHERS LIMITED

## TO THE READER

**Dear Mum, I Miss You** is a story set in Britain during the early years of the Second World War. Grace Williams and the other characters in the book are made up, but the setting is real. The retreat of the British army from Dunkirk in 1940, for example, actually happened. So the story is not just exciting; it will also tell you what life was like during an extraordinary period in our history.

*Stewart Ross*

*For the staff and pupils of the Junior Department of the Lady Eleanor Holles School, Hampton Hill, Middlesex.*

This edition first published 2006 by Evans Brothers Limited,
2A Portman Mansions, Chiltern Street, London W1U 6NR

British Library Cataloguing in Publication Data
Ross, Stewart
Dear Mum, I miss you (Flashbacks)
1. World War, 1939-1945 Social Aspects Great Britain Juvenile fiction
2. Children's stories
I. Title
823.9'14(J)

Reprinted 2010

Printed in China

978 0237 53149 2

# CONTENTS

| | | |
|---|---|---|
| | NO ONE WILL BE SAFE… | **page 7** |
| 1 | THE SIREN | **page 9** |
| 2 | MISSING, PRESUMED DEAD | **page 15** |
| 3 | THE BLITZ | **page 23** |
| 4 | AUNT EMILY | **page 29** |
| 5 | SILENT SADNESS | **page 35** |
| 6 | THE STRANGER | **page 43** |

**HISTORY FILE**

| | |
|---|---|
| Britain at War | **page 49** |
| New Words | **page 52** |
| Time Line | **page 54** |

# No one will be safe…

BRITAIN AT WAR

The British people were not surprised when their country entered the Second World War on 3 September 1939. But they were certainly frightened. Experts said that no one would be safe. They predicted that German bombers would destroy British cities with high explosives and fire, and possibly try to kill people with poison gas.

EMERGENCY PLANS

Before the war started, the government took steps to protect people from air raids. Everyone, including babies, was given a gas mask and told to keep it handy at all times. Air-raid shelters, large and small, were built to protect people from bomb blasts. Important buildings were protected with sandbags. Hospitals, the police and fire services drew up emergency plans.

At night, all streetlights were switched off and windows had to be blacked out. This was to make it difficult for enemy bombers to find their targets. Wardens had the job of seeing that these air-raid precautions were carried out.

## ON THE LOOKOUT

On the coast, lookouts and radar operators watched for enemy aircraft. When bombers were spotted, the news was passed inland. In the cities, air-raid sirens warned people that an attack was expected...

# CHAPTER ONE

# THE SIREN

The sound came from somewhere near the river. It started as a low growl and rose to a long, mournful wail.

Grace Williams looked up from her homework. She had lived in London all her life and was used to fire sirens. After a quick glance out of the window to see if the smoke was visible from the fifth-floor flat, she pushed back a lock of curly brown hair from her forehead and went back to her geography notes.

But something was wrong.

After holding its high note for a few seconds, the siren had fallen back to a growl. Then it rose again to a scream. On and on the noise went, rising and falling like the howl of a wolf.

Grace felt a shiver run through her body.

She put down her pen. What on earth...? Surely it couldn't be an air-raid warning already. The war had only started yesterday. She got up and stood by the window. As she gazed over the roofs of Battersea glowing in the warm light of a September evening, she became aware of another sound.

'Grace! *Grace!*' The call was even more urgent than the wail of the siren.

Grace heard footsteps hurrying down the passage from the kitchen. The door flew open and her mother burst into the room. Her face was as white as the flour clinging to the front of her apron.

'Grace!' she cried. 'Can't you hear it?'

Grace stood open-mouthed. She had not seen her mother look this worried since her father had gone away to join the army.

'It's only a practice, isn't it?' she mumbled.

'*Practice!* Good God, Grace, have you forgotten we're at war? Now put on your gas mask and get down to the cellar before we're blown to smithereens!'

It was the first time Grace had heard her mother swear. Shocked, she pulled her gas mask out from under her bed, tugged it on over her glasses and, without another word, followed her mother down to the cellar.

Grace's family rented a four-room flat at the top of Albion Villas, a large Victorian building at the corner of Hanover Street and Victoria Terrace. It was taller than the houses around it and from her window Grace could see the billowing chimneys of Battersea Power Station and the brown waters of the Thames beyond.

The power station worried Grace's mother. 'It's bound to be a target for the bombers,' she told Grace on the evening that Mr Jeffreys, the local air-raid warden, checked their gas masks. 'Even if we don't get gassed, we'll be blown up by bombs meant for the power station...'

The remark had started an argument. Grace's mother wanted her to join the thousands of other children who would be evacuated from London if a war started.

'You'd be so much safer in the countryside, my love,' she pleaded.

Grace refused. She wasn't a clingy child. It was just that, now her father was away, she didn't want to leave her mother on her own. Although Grace was only twelve, she felt strangely protective towards her mum. Not that Mrs Williams needed looking after. She was twenty-nine years old and had recently started as a full-time supervisor at Walkers Knitwear of Fulham, which now made parachutes for the RAF.

Even so, Grace wouldn't change her mind. She was not going to leave London and live in some draughty farmhouse miles from anywhere with people she didn't even know.

• • • • •

Sitting beside Grace in the cellar of Albion Villas, her mother tried again.

It had been an hour since the siren had gone off. As no bombs had fallen, they realised it had been a false alarm and had removed their gas masks.

'Just because we weren't bombed this time, darling, it doesn't mean it won't happen,' she began.

'I know,' said Grace absent-mindedly. She was wondering how she was going to manage to finish her homework on time.

'So what about going somewhere safe, just for a little while—'

'*Mum!*' interrupted Grace. 'I've already said I'm not leaving! Why are you so keen to get rid of me?'

'Oh, don't be so silly, Grace! I just want to send you away from the bombing, that's all.' She tried a new approach. 'You could stay with Aunt Emily...'

'Not on your life!' Grace replied crossly.

Grace had never met Aunt Emily, her father's unmarried eldest sister. Aunt Emily lived alone in Honiton, Devon, and never wrote, not even at Christmas. Grace had once asked her dad what she was like.

'Oh, Emily's nice enough,' he had replied. 'Just a bit stuck in the past, that's all.'

The last thing that Grace wanted was to go and live with some old-fashioned fogey in the middle of nowhere. No, she thought, I'm not going to Aunt Emily's. Not even if the whole of London is bombed as flat as a pancake.

# Chapter two

# Missing, presumed dead

That autumn, Grace found herself living in an unreal world. Where was the war everyone had said would be so terrible? It seemed to be happening only in the newspapers or on the radio, not in the skies above London or even in the fields of France.

Like everyone else, Grace's family still blacked out their windows at night so that enemy bombers couldn't see their lights. The air-raid sirens went off from time to time, too. But just as on that first warm evening in September, no planes came.

Grace didn't always take her heavy gas mask to school. Sometimes, when the teachers checked, she was sent home to collect it. Walking back past the empty air-raid shelters and government posters, she imagined she was on a film set. Everything looked like a city in wartime, but there was no actual danger.

Not then, anyway.

• • • • •

At the beginning of the autumn term, Grace's school was half-empty because so many pupils had been evacuated. The staff were more relaxed and Grace's teacher, Mrs Filton, treated her almost like a friend. Mrs Filton's son, Philip, was an engineer on *HMS Zulu*. Mrs Filton called him 'our secret war hero' and pinned up his picture next to the blackboard.

By December, there had still been no serious air raids. Most of the evacuees gradually returned home. The school was soon back to its usual, bustling self again. Mrs Filton became more strict and even took down the picture of her son. It wasn't appropriate any more, she said.

The return of the evacuees had its good side, though. Grace's mother didn't mention Aunt Emily any more and Grace enjoyed seeing her old friends again, especially Mary Timpson. Mary had been sent to a farm in Warwickshire. The farmer had let her milk the cows and even ride Plodder, his old Shire horse. Secretly, Grace was a bit jealous.

At Christmas Grace's dad came home on leave. Dressed in his smart new uniform, he looked taller and stronger than Grace remembered. He moved differently, too. Instead of shuffling along,

as he did when he worked in the bank, he now walked briskly with his back as straight as a broom handle.

'Proper sergeant major, aren't you, Frank!' said Grace's mother proudly, watching her husband carry his bulky kitbag into the flat as if it were no heavier than a handbag.

'Bit fitter than I was, Barbara!' he replied, throwing his kitbag on to the sofa. 'Not a sergeant yet, though. But getting there.' He pointed to the white stripe sewn on to his sleeve. 'Not bad, eh? Lance-corporal after less than a year.'

'You got promoted? You never told me.' Grace's mother tried to look cross.

'Only happened last week, Barbara. Thought I'd keep it as a surprise.'

'It *is* a surprise,' she smiled, putting her arms round his neck and kissing him. 'A fantastic one! Well done, Frank – and welcome home!'

The Williams family had a wonderful Christmas. The time Grace enjoyed most was going to the cinema with her dad, just the two of them. On the way home, he told Grace funny stories about army life, talking to her as if she was another adult and using words she didn't really understand. She felt so proud of him, so grown up, so happy.

19

Looking back, Grace thought of the day her father returned to his regiment as the day that her war really started.

In February he wrote to say he was being sent to France. After reading the letter, Grace's mother turned pale and burst into tears.

Grace was upset and confused. 'But there isn't a war in France,' she said, trying hard not to cry herself.

Her mother dabbed at her eyes with a handkerchief. 'Sorry, Grace. It's silly of me. I know there isn't any fighting in France. But I'm frightened that there will be. And when it comes, your dad will be in the thick of it.'

She covered her face with her hands and started crying again. 'I hate this war!' she sobbed. 'Oh, Grace! I hate it so much!'

Grace's father wrote home regularly. Grace read his long, chatty letters over and over again until she knew them all by heart.

But suddenly, in May, the letters stopped.

The Germans had launched an attack into France, driving back the British and French armies. The British, suffering heavy casualties, retreated to the French port of Dunkirk. The government called on all sea-going ships to rescue them and somehow the remainder of the army was brought home.

Every day Grace and her mother anxiously scoured the lists printed in the newspapers, naming men who had been killed, wounded or captured. Lance-corporal Frank Williams was never mentioned. But no letters came, either.

Then, one Saturday afternoon in the middle of June, a telegram was delivered by a man in uniform.

'It is with great regret,' Mrs Williams read in a quiet, trembling voice, 'that His Majesty's Government begs to inform you that Lance-corporal Frank Williams has been reported missing, presumed dead.'

# CHAPTER THREE

# THE BLITZ

People react differently to bad news. Grace's mother simply refused to accept it. In her mind the important word in the telegram was 'missing'.

She didn't weep after she had read the telegram. She just sat bolt upright at the kitchen table, her face as hard as marble, and repeated in a strange, strained voice, 'Don't worry, Grace. He'll be back. He's only missing, you know. Only missing.'

Grace's mother never once uttered the words 'presumed dead', not even when she heard from Captain Wilmot, her husband's commanding officer.

He wrote a kind but ominous letter, saying that he had last seen Frank, 'a man of great courage', helping wounded comrades on the beach at Dunkirk. He did not appear to have made it to one of the rescue boats and the Germans did not mention him in their prisoner lists. One of his friends thought he had been killed by a bomb.

It was as if a curtain had closed off part of Grace's mother's mind. She went to work as if nothing had happened. And when anyone asked how Frank was, she just replied, 'He's all right, thanks. Mind you, I'm not sure where he is. You know what men are like about keeping in touch.'

Grace could not share her mother's hopes. She knew what 'presumed dead' meant – her dad would almost certainly never come home. But when she tried to talk about her worries and fears with her mother, she always got the same reply: 'He's only missing, Grace. Don't worry, he'll be back.' This left Grace with a painful feeling of loneliness, as if part of her mother was missing, too.

Grace's school friends were all very kind, especially Mary. But Grace knew that they didn't understand. How could they? No one else in her class had a close relative who'd been killed or even wounded. Only Mrs Filton seemed to know how Grace really felt.

Grace often stayed behind after school and talked about her father while her class teacher tidied up and got things ready for the next day.

Every now and again, her teacher would look up and say kindly, 'I understand, my dear. I know just what it's like.'

Much later, Grace learned that Mrs Filton's son's ship, *HMS Zulu*, had been sunk at about the time of Dunkirk. There were no survivors.

Grace felt as if the war had played a cruel trick on her, first pretending it wasn't there, then hitting her with terrible force, just when she believed she was safe. Her loneliness lasted until halfway through the summer holidays, when the Blitz finally came to London.

It began shortly after Dunkirk, when a few German planes struggled through Britain's defences to bomb the capital in daylight. Soon, larger and larger formations came, droning in from the east like swarms of huge, angry hornets.

The air-raid sirens went off every morning, and Grace spent her days curled up with a book in the cellar of Albion Villas. When the all-clear sounded, she hurried up to the flat and looked out over the city. Fire-engine bells clanged in the distance and clouds of smoke hung over the burning docks. But the west of the city, including Battersea, remained largely unharmed.

School did not re-open on time. Many pupils had been evacuated a second time and it was considered too dangerous for those who remained to gather together in one place. When the enemy switched to night-time raids, however, the authorities felt that it was safe again and the autumn term finally began. Meanwhile, the bombing had spread across the city towards Battersea.

• • • • •

Grace was now no longer alone in her misery. Each morning, exhausted after sleepless nights in shelters and basements, her school friends told of what they had seen and heard. June Smith's uncle died when a blazing warehouse collapsed. A direct hit on a corrugated iron shelter in Lucy Allot's garden killed her and all her family. Brothers, sisters, parents, teachers, friends – no one was safe.

Once again, Grace's mother tried to persuade her to leave the city. She told her daughter that Aunt Emily had sent word that Grace was welcome to come and stay in Devon at any time.

Again, Grace refused.

'I can't leave now, Mum,' she explained, 'not after what's happened.'

Her mother had grown thinner in recent months. Sounding very tired, she asked, 'What's happened, love?'

'Oh, Mum!' sighed Grace, trying not to cry. 'You know. Dad not being here any more.'

'He's only miss...' For the first time Grace's mother did not finish the sentence. Instead, she took Grace in her arms and said quietly, 'OK, love. Stay if you want to. But think it over, please. For my sake.'

• • • • •

In the end, Grace's mind was made up for her. Mr Jeffreys, the air-raid warden, had recently persuaded Grace and her mother to spend their nights in Clapham Common tube station. Returning home early one morning, they turned into Hanover Street and stopped in their tracks. Grace stared in disbelief.

The street was littered with pieces of brick and timber. Several houses were still burning. On the corner, where Albion Villas had stood, lay a jagged pile of smoking rubble.

# Chapter four

# Aunt Emily

Apart from the clothes they were wearing and the overnight bag they had with them at the air-raid shelter, Grace and her mother lost everything. They didn't mind too much about goods they could buy again, such as furniture and bedding. What really hurt was losing things they could never replace – family photographs, souvenirs and, most precious of all, Frank's last letters. The bomb that had destroyed Albion Villas had also destroyed their past.

Later, as they sat drinking mugs of tea in a rest centre, Grace's mother said quietly, 'Memories. That's all I've got left. Just memories.'

Grace placed her hand over her mother's. 'You've got me, Mum. I'm still here.'

Grace's mother smiled weakly. 'Of course, my love,' she said. 'Thank God. And you've got me, too, don't forget. I suppose that's all that really matters.' She stared into her mug for a few moments. 'But if anything happened to you, I don't think I could go on.'

'But nothing's going to happen to me,' replied Grace, giving her hand a squeeze.

Her mother took a sip of tea. 'Nothing's certain, Grace. Not in war it isn't.'

It was then that Grace realised what she had to do. If she remained in the burning, blasted city, her mother would not have a moment free from anxiety and fear. No, like it or not, as soon as her mother found somewhere to live, Grace had to go and stay with Aunt Emily.

Vera Armitage, one of Grace's mother's friends from work, said she could have a room at her house for as long as she wanted. She accepted the offer gratefully. Four days later, having written a quick note to Aunt Emily saying when Grace was due to arrive, she took Grace to the station and put her on the train to Honiton.

Grace stood waving out of the carriage window long after her mother had disappeared from sight. As the train gathered speed though the suburbs, she closed the window and sat down. There was no one else in her compartment. There was no one else in her life, either. Overcome with misery and loneliness, she threw herself into the padded corner of the seat and wept.

It was almost dark when the train steamed into Honiton Station. Taking her small suitcase from the rack, Grace stepped down on to the platform and looked about her. Apart from the departing passengers, the only other person in sight was a rather severe-looking woman standing near the ticket barrier. She was wearing a heavy overcoat and an old-fashioned black hat.

Oh, dear! thought Grace. That must be Aunt Emily. She put down her suitcase and waved cheerily in the woman's direction. The woman did not move.

Grace walked slowly towards the muffled figure. 'Aunt Emily?' she asked nervously.

'Aye,' came the reply from beneath the woman's funereal hat.

As Grace bent forward for a kiss, she noticed with a pang of sorrow that her aunt had the same dark eyes as her father.

Aunt Emily took half a step back and held out her hand. 'Evening, niece Grace,' she said in a slow, suspicious-sounding Devonshire accent. 'Journey all right?'

Grace shook her aunt's gloved hand. The fingers felt soft and plump, like sausages. 'Fine, thank you,' she said uncertainly.

Without another word, Aunt Emily turned and walked with short, quick steps through the ticket barrier.

Grace felt the grey wave of loneliness rising up inside her again. Picking up her suitcase, she walked through the gloomy booking hall into the road beyond.

'This way,' directed her aunt, setting off at a brisk walk along the deserted street.

Grace followed in silence. She wondered whether her aunt had ever held a conversation in her life.

● ● ● ● ●

Aunt Emily lived at Christmas Cottage, a small semi-detached house about half a mile from the centre of the town. When they arrived, she lit an oil lamp and showed Grace to her room. 'Not like London,' she said as she opened the door.

Grace glanced around the room. The floor was made from uneven wooden boards. A high metal bed covered with a chequered quilt stood against one wall. Opposite was an ancient oak wardrobe. On a table next to the low window stood a candlestick, a washbasin and a tall enamel jug.

'It's lovely!' exclaimed Grace. 'Just like a picture in a storybook!'

'Wouldn't know,' her aunt replied mysteriously.

Grace watched her close the faded blue curtains and light the candle. Why won't she speak to me? she wondered. If I'm not welcome, why did she invite me?

'Supper in ten minutes,' said her aunt. She blew out the match she had used to light the candle and turned to go. She paused by the door and gave Grace a strange, mournful look. Grace was sure she wanted to say something.

But no words came.

Aunt Emily closed the door quietly behind her and went downstairs to prepare supper.

# CHAPTER FIVE

# SILENT SADNESS

Supper was the best meal Grace had eaten for ages. Fresh food was in short supply in London, but not in Devonshire, it seemed. At least, not at Aunt Emily's. Grace came downstairs to find her plate piled high with bacon and eggs, and she wolfed down the lot as if she hadn't eaten for a week.

'Big appetite,' observed Aunt Emily.

'I was starving,' Grace replied, scraping up the last bit of egg yolk with her fork. 'The bacon was really good.'

'Local,' said her aunt. She was only halfway through her own, smaller meal.

Grace put down her knife and fork and looked at her aunt across the table. 'This really is very kind of you, Aunt Emily,' she said politely.

Her aunt glanced up then went on with her meal.

Grace tried again. 'I mean, having me to stay like this. It must be a nuisance for you.'

'Only normal,' replied her aunt, helping herself to the salt.

Grace wanted to scream. I can't live like this, she thought. I'll go mad if she doesn't talk to me. 'What do you do all day, aunt?' she asked in desperation.

Aunt Emily waited until she had cut the rind off a piece of bacon, then replied, 'Just the usual.'

Grace let out a long, loud sigh.

'Niece Grace,' Aunt Emily said firmly, but without anger, 'you're welcome here. But don't expect no conversation. I'm no talker. Just you remember that and we'll jog along fine. So there's an end to it.'

And there was an end to it. Grace and her aunt exchanged no more than half a dozen words for the rest of the evening. Grace helped wash up and put things away, then said good-night and went up to her room.

After unpacking her few things, Grace washed and got into bed.

She lay there with her eyes closed, listening to the sound of the wind tugging at the thatch overhead. It reminded her of the sirens at home. The loneliness and pain of the past few months crept over her like a dark tide. She thought of her

mother and wondered if she was safe. 'Oh, no!' she whispered into the darkness. 'What have I done?'

Unable to sleep, Grace lit the candle and took out the pen and notepaper her mother had given her before she left London. She sat on the edge of the bed and opened the pad. Across the first sheet her mother had written: *For my darling daughter Grace – enjoy your holiday!*

Grace's eyes filled with tears. Turning to the second sheet, she rested the pad on her knee and began to write:

*Dear Mum, I miss you!*

The next morning, after a hearty breakfast, Grace asked what she should do.

'School,' replied her aunt. 'Starts eight-thirty, up the street, on the right.'

Grace didn't realise she'd have to start at the local school so soon. With a heavy heart, she walked slowly down the street and entered the playground.

'Another 'vacuee!' someone shouted.

Grace was immediately surrounded by a crowd of children wanting to know about the London Blitz. Had she seen a bomb go off? Was it

scary? Was it true that people in air-raid shelters would rather wet their pants than go outside during a raid?

Grace answered as best she could before the bell rang for lessons.

The day was better than she thought it would be. The teachers were kind, and although one or two pupils teased her about her accent, most were friendly.

At break-time she made friends with Jane Barnecutt, a large, rosy-cheeked girl of about her own age. When Grace told her where she was staying, Jane said something that surprised her.

'Miss Williams? She be a sad one, Grace. Ate up with silent sadness, they say, for years and years and years.'

Grace turned the remark over in her mind. If I knew what this silent sadness was, she thought, I might be able to help. Then, perhaps, Aunt Emily will not be quite so defensive towards me...

● ● ● ● ●

Returning home after her third day at school, Grace found Aunt Emily seated at the kitchen table polishing something. As Grace entered, she hurriedly slipped it into a drawer, but not before Grace had seen what it was.

'Hello, Aunt Emily!' called Grace. 'What were you cleaning?'

'Trinket,' her aunt replied awkwardly.

'It looked like a cap badge to me,' said Grace. 'Like the one dad wore.'

Aunt Emily sat absolutely still for a few moments, than asked slowly, 'Why did you say "wore", niece Grace? Don't he wear it no more?'

I don't believe it, thought Grace. She doesn't know. 'Didn't you receive Mum's letter?'

Her aunt looked embarrassed. 'Might 'ave. Might not. Never learned reading. My neighbour read me the one about your coming down.'

'Oh, Aunt Emily!' Grace exclaimed. 'If only I'd known! There's something you should know...'

As calmly as she could, Grace explained about the awful 'missing, presumed dead' telegram and about the bombing of Albion Mansions. When she had finished, she looked up and saw that Aunt Emily's eyes were filled with tears.

'Poor girl!' she said kindly. 'Poor Frank, too. That makes two of them, then.'

Grace frowned. 'Two of them? What do you mean?'

'Your dad never told you my story?'

Grace shook her head.

'Then I reckons I'll have to tell you myself.'

# CHAPTER SIX

# THE STRANGER

Aunt Emily's story was one of the saddest Grace had ever heard.

On Christmas Eve, 1915, when she was just seventeen, Emily became engaged to Billy, a young soldier home on leave from the First World War. The days they spent together were the happiest of her life. But they slipped by all too quickly. In early January Billy was called back to his regiment. Seven months later, he was killed at the Battle of the Somme.

Heartbroken, Emily was kept going only by the knowledge that she was carrying Billy's child. The baby, a healthy, curly-haired girl with deep brown eyes, was born in October. Emily did not have a photograph of Billy. Apart from her engagement ring and the spare cap badge he had given her, the baby girl was all she had to remind her of him.

Six months later, her daughter died of meningitis.

'And after that,' said Aunt Emily, wiping her eyes with a small lace handkerchief, 'I ain't been one for company and talking. I've had my life, you see. It ended when my baby was took away.'

• • • • •

Grace sat in silence, too upset even to notice the tears rolling down her own cheeks.

Eventually, she said, 'I'm so sorry. Because of losing Dad, I understand a little bit. But the baby… What was her name?'

'Can't you guess, niece? She was called Grace. That's why it's so hard you being here, with your brown eyes and all. She would have looked just like you.'

● ● ● ● ●

Life at Christmas Cottage was much easier now. A bond of affection had grown up between Grace and her aunt, making their relationship warmer and more relaxed. Grace put on weight and her wavy brown hair, which had grown lank and dull since her father went missing, regained its old lustre. Aunt Emily still didn't say much, but she liked to hear how Grace was getting on at school and listened eagerly when she read out her mother's weekly letters.

The news was bitter-sweet. Grace loved the gossipy stories about the girls at Walkers Knitwear and Vera Armitage's dreadful cooking. But reports of the terrible bombing – night after night – made her worry about her mother. It also brought back painful memories of crowded shelters, of sirens and Albion Villas in ruins. Images of her father floated into her mind, too. Dad returning from the bank... showing off in his new uniform... lying bleeding on the beach at Dunkirk...

• • • • •

Mrs Williams' letter of 21 October was shorter than usual. It said simply that she had a surprise for Grace: she had time off work and was coming down to Honiton for a few days. As Grace read the next sentence, her joy turned to horror: *We will catch the 10.36 from Waterloo.*

Grace's mind filled with anger and guilt. 'We' could mean only one thing. Her mother had found someone else – already! How could she?

'I should never have left her alone,' Grace told herself.

The London train was on time. Standing on the platform beside Aunt Emily, Grace watched the passengers getting off. Her mother was one of the last. Seeing Grace, she gave a cheery wave then turned to help a man with a walking stick down the steps.

Grace felt sick. She couldn't believe it. How could Mum do this to her? Disgusted, she watched the man steady himself, then take her mother's hand.

Grace froze. The gesture looked somehow familiar.

Then she realised.

'Dad!' she screamed, tearing down the platform. 'Dad! Dad! Dad!'

● ● ● ● ●

Over tea at Christmas Cottage, Grace's father explained what had happened. A Red Cross worker had found him, unconscious and badly wounded, lying on the beach at Dunkirk. He was brought home in a coma. His identity disc was missing, so no one knew who he was. Worse still, when he eventually recovered consciousness, he had lost his memory.

He remained in hospital for many weeks. Gradually, his strength returned – but not his memory. Then, one night, he dreamed about his wedding. When he awoke, the image remained in his mind. One of the doctors wrote down the description of the church, found out where it was and traced his patient's name and address. But his letter to Mrs Barbara Williams at Flat 12, Albion Villas was returned. The postman had scrawled *'House Bombed Out'* across the envelope.

'Anyway, to cut a long story short,' said Mr Williams, 'the army soon found out where Barbara was living and, well, here we are.'

Aunt Emily poured him another cup of tea. 'To my thinking, Frank,' she said, 'London's no place for you and Barbara. Not with all them bombs. Why don't you stay here a while?'

Frank Williams turned to his wife.

'It's very kind of you, Emily,' she said. 'We'd love to, but only if—'

'No "ifs", Barbara,' interrupted Aunt Emily. 'I've room enough. And Honiton ain't so bad, eh, Grace?'

'It's *wonderful!*' laughed Grace. 'With everyone here it's the best place in the world!'

# BRITAIN AT WAR

AIR-RAID SHELTERS

At first, Grace and her mother sheltered in the basement of their block of flats. Basements were fairly safe, but those sheltering in them could be trapped if the building above collapsed. Later, they went to Clapham Common underground station. Tube stations, especially those on the Northern Line (which was the deepest), were the safest form of air-raid shelter and were very crowded.

Grace's friend Lucy Allot and her family were killed while taking refuge in a corrugated iron shelter in their garden. This type of shelter, known as a Morrison Shelter, was cheap and quick to put up. But it gave protection only if a high-explosive bomb landed some distance away.

BLACKOUT

Mr Jeffreys, the ARP (Air-Raid Protection) warden who looked after Albion Villas, made sure that no lights were visible from the street. Most people blacked out their windows with heavy curtains.

## JOINING THE ARMED FORCES

In March 1939, Frank Williams joined the army as a volunteer. Two months later, the government introduced 'conscription'. This meant that all young men had to be prepared to join the armed forces or do other vital war work. Later, women were also conscripted.

## DUNKIRK

In May 1940, a sudden German attack in France drove back the British, French and Belgian armies towards the Channel. They gathered on the beaches near the port of Dunkirk and the British government asked everyone with sea-going boats to help rescue them. Remarkably, the fleet of warships and small boats managed to pick up over 330,000 men (including Lance-corporal Frank Williams) and bring them back to Britain.

## EVACUATION

There was no law to say that children had to be evacuated from Britain's cities. But many parents wanted their children sent somewhere safe. Some, like Mrs Williams, made their own evacuation arrangements. Others used the government scheme, which took place just before the war broke out. Some children, like Grace, went on their own; others were accompanied by their mothers. When there were few air raids, many evacuees returned home. There was a second evacuation after Dunkirk and a third when missiles began falling on London in 1944.

## FOOD SHORTAGES

Much of Britain's food comes from abroad by sea. During the war, enemy warships attacked the vessels bringing food, and supplies ran low. To make sure everyone had enough to eat, the government set limits on the amount of food each person could buy. This was called 'rationing'. Bacon and eggs were rationed, which is why Grace was so surprised to find her plate piled high with them at Aunt Emily's. Her aunt got round the rationing by buying food direct from a local farmer – she would have been in trouble if anyone had found out!

## WOMEN AT WORK

When Mrs Williams started as a full-time supervisor at Walkers Knitwear, it was her first paid job since Grace had been born. Before the war she had been a full-time housewife. Like many other women, when war seemed certain she had taken a job to help with the war effort. Women were needed to do the jobs that men had done before they joined the armed forces. In March 1941, the government said that all young women (except those with children living at home) had to be prepared to do war work.

# NEW WORDS

**Air raid**  An attack by enemy aircraft, usually bombers.

**Air-raid shelter** A place where people could shelter from a bomb attack. Many were underground. They were usually made of steel or concrete.

**Armed forces**  The army, navy and air force.

**Blitz**  The heavy bombing of a city. 'Blitz' comes from the German word *Blitzkrieg*, which means 'lightning war'.

**Casualty**  Someone who is injured or wounded.

**Coma**  Being unconscious for a long time.

**Conscript**  To require someone to join the forces or do other war work.

**Evacuate**  To move people to a safe place, usually out of towns and cities.

**Evacuee**  Someone who was evacuated.

**Formation**  A number of planes flying together.

**Invade**  To move into another country by force. In 1940 the Germans invaded France and planned to invade Britain.

**Lance-corporal**  A rank in the army. Lance-corporal was the first rank above an ordinary soldier, or private.

**Meningitis** A disease of the brain and spine that can be fatal.

**Power station** A place where electricity is made.

**Promote** To give someone a more important position at work or in the armed forces.

**Radar** A way of finding distant metal objects, such as planes, by bouncing radio waves off them. The word 'radar' comes from radio detection and ranging.

**Rationing** Limiting the amount of food people could buy and sharing it out equally.

**Red Cross** An organisation that looks after the sick and injured.

**Regiment** One of the main divisions of soldiers in the army.

**Sergeant** A rank in the army above lance-corporal and corporal, but below an officer.

**Shire horse** A large horse used for farm work.

**Telegram** A type of letter that is delivered very quickly.

**Warden** Someone who looks after others. An air-raid warden, for example, helped people during air raids.

**Warehouse** A building where goods are stored.

• • • • •

# TIME LINE

**1936** Britain starts building air-raid shelters.

**1939** **September** First evacuation of mothers and children from large cities. War begins. Blackout started. First air raids.

**1940** **January** Government introduces food rationing.

**May** German forces invade France, Luxembourg, Belgium and Holland.

**May–June** British army rescued from Dunkirk.

**June** Second evacuation of mothers and children from large cities.

Government introduces clothes rationing.

**July–Sept** Battle of Britain.

**September** London Blitz begins.

**1941** **March** Women have to sign up to do war work.

**December** USA joins the war.

**1943** Many evacuees return home.

**1944** **July** Missiles hit London.

Third evacuation of mothers and children from London.

**1945** **May** War ends in Europe. Remaining evacuees start to return home.

**August** War ends in Far East.